# The Fairy in the Kettle

**PAULINE TAIT**

ILLUSTRATED BY DEBBIE BELLABY

Matador
9 Priory Business Park,
Wistow Road, Kibworth Beauchamp,
Leicestershire. LE8 0RX
Tel: 0116 279 2299
Email: books@troubador.co.uk
Web: www.troubador.co.uk/matador
Twitter: @matadorbooks

ISBN 978 1785891 496

British Library Cataloguing in Publication Data.
A catalogue record for this book is available from the British Library.

Typeset in Palatino by Troubador Publishing Ltd, Leicester, UK

Matador is an imprint of Troubador Publishing Ltd

Leona Rose was sure that she was the happiest fairy in all of Fairyland. She had great friends, a wonderful family and lived in a beautiful little village deep in the heart of Bramble Glen.

She was also sure that she had the best house
in all of Fairyland, although her friends and
family strongly disagreed with her!

You see, Leona lives in an old, round cast iron kettle that she found many summers ago while she was flying deep in the woods. She could still remember the struggle she and her three best friends, Tilly, Robbie and Toby had as they tried to fly the very heavy kettle back to their village.

But when they placed it in her favourite spot under the old oak tree, Leona knew that all their efforts had been worth it.

The kettle was beautifully decorated with the colours from the woods around the village. She had squashed bramble juice to stain the inside of the kettle walls pale purple to match her wings. The soft twigs from the willow tree made a very comfortable bed, which she covered in layers of dried pink and white rose petals, making it very soft and cosy.

In winter, she used the red leaves from the copper beech tree to line the floor

and in the summer she used the lovely fresh green leaves she gathered from around the woods.

Leona loved living in her kettle and often had her friends and family round for some fresh spring water and berries, but if it started to rain her visitors would leave very quickly without even stopping to say goodbye.

But Leona would just laugh because she loved it when it rained. To Leona, listening to the sound of the raindrops landing on the kettle was like listening to music, and every shower of rain played a different tune.

She would dance around inside her kettle creating new dance steps to each shower of rain. When the rain was fast and heavy she would practise her quick steps and, when it was just a little light shower, she would practise her ballet.

However, to everyone else the raindrops landing on the kettle was the most annoying noise they had ever heard.

One evening, Leona and her friends were flying over Buttercup Brook. They were playing with the swallows as they flew low over the water when it started to rain very heavily. Heavy rain can damage the fairies' delicate little wings, so they flew home quickly.

As darkness fell the rain got heavier and a strong wind began to blow. Before long a storm was raging over the village. All the fairies, except Leona, had been asleep in the closed flower heads that they snuggled into each night but, as the flowers began to blow back and forth in the strong wind, the fairies were no longer safe.

The fairies had to leave
their little flowers and
huddle together under the
roots of the old oak tree.

The howling wind and driving rain was sweeping the little fairies off their feet. Their little wings were feeling battered and they were becoming more miserable as each minute passed.

However, the noise of the lashing rain against Leona's precious kettle meant she couldn't hear the wind and she was completely unaware of the storm raging outside.

She was dancing around in her kettle, delighted that the rain was lasting so long as she created one wonderful dance after another.

She twirled and twirled around her kettle, humming a tune and pretending she was on a stage and everyone had come just to see the magnificent Leona, world-class dancer and prima ballerina.

She danced and twirled and danced and twirled and danced and twirled and *crashed* as every fairy in the village flew down the spout of her precious kettle one after the other.

She was horrified to see them so cold and wet and grabbed some lovely pink and white rose petals that she had neatly stacked in the corner. As the fairies dried themselves with the rose petals, Leona gathered some berries and nuts from her larder for her weary guests to eat.

The fairies were so relieved
not to hear the howling
wind that the noise of
the rain hammering
off the outside of the
kettle was actually
not so bad anymore,
and the fairies began
to join Leona in
dancing to the sound
of the raindrops. As
the hours passed,
the little village in
Bramble Glen was
battered by one of
the worst storms in its
history but the fairies
were blissfully unaware
of what was going on
outside.

They were having the best party the village had ever had and from that night on, whenever there was a storm, Leona's kettle would fill up as all the fairies in the village gathered, knowing they were safe, warm and happy together.

Lightning Source UK Ltd.
Milton Keynes UK
UKRC02n1925260816
281608UK00001B/1